BABYLON

First published March 1982 by
André Deutsch Limited
105 Great Russell Street London WC1
Second impression November 1982
Third impression July 1984

Colour origination by DOT Gradations Limited,
Chelmsford, Essex,
Phototypeset by Tradespools Limited,
Frome, Somerset.
Printed in Hong Kong by Colorcraft Ltd.

British Library Cataloguing in Publication Data
Walsh, Jill Paton
Babylon.
I. Title
823′ .914[J]   PZ7.P2735

ISBN 0-233-97362-1

First Published in the United States of America 1982
Library of Congress Number 81-67625.

Babylon

Story by Jill Paton Walsh

Pictures by Jennifer Northway

ANDRE DEUTSCH

Behind the houses where Dulcie lives there is a railway viaduct.

Nothing grows in Dulcie's back yard, any time of the year, because the viaduct keeps out the sun. But if Dulcie looks up she sees grass, like a green velvet ribbon, on top of the dirty brick wall, and a thorn bush with white blossom in spring.

In summer there are long-legged purple flowers up there, that turn all soft and downy before the blackberries come on the bramble bush.

"If that a railway, why no trains been coming?" Dulcie asked her mother.

"That railway been closed down this long while," her mother told her.

Dulcie's friend David lives in a flat half way up the tower block. From David's window you can see the viaduct going along through the streets and houses. The rails have been taken up and so have the sleepers. The viaduct is growing a wildflower garden all along.

"I really would like to walk up on down there," said Dulcie.

"I'll take you," said David. "We find a way."

They went down Railway Lane, beside the arches. Some of the arches are used as workshops. They have big wooden doors built across them.

Beams on the doors give footholds.
  Dulcie climbed up to the top of one of the doors. But it was
a long way from the top of the door to the top of the viaduct.
"Come down, Dulcie, you gonna fall," David called to her.
She came down.

A way further there is a junkyard. An old bus is in the junkyard, right beside the viaduct. It has big blue eyes on the front to see the way. Dulcie and David went up to the top deck, and looked through the broken window at the viaduct.

"We get a plank of wood," said David, "and we put it across and walk over. Easy."

"A plank would be good and steep," said Dulcie.

"Not too much," said David.

They looked all over the dump, but they couldn't find a plank long enough.

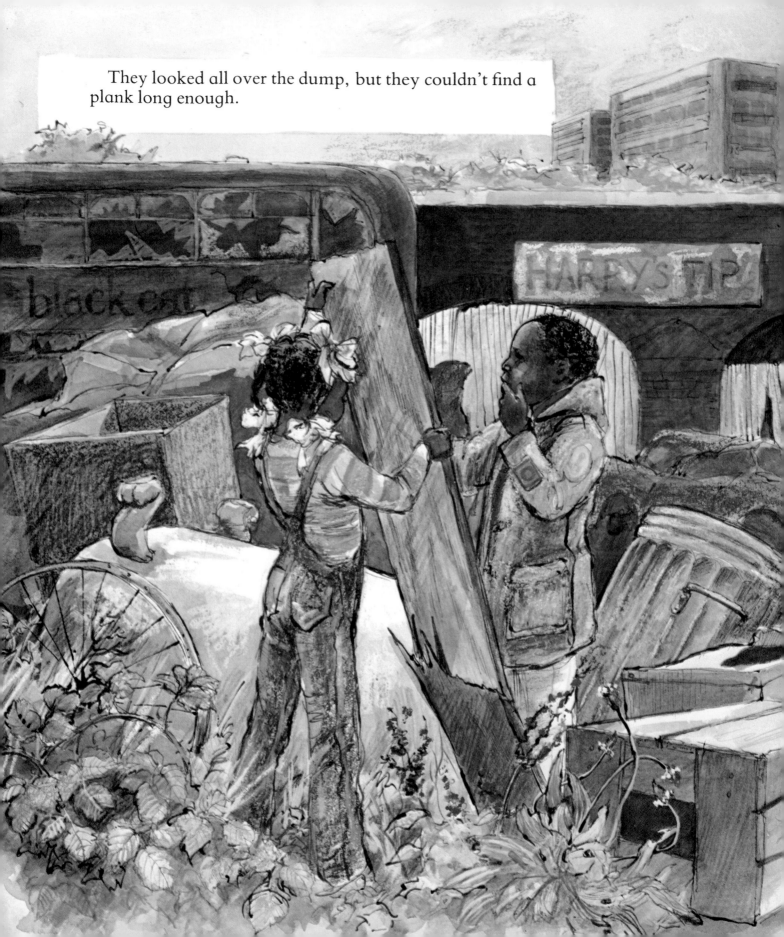

A way further, and they found an open arch, piled full of old oildrums.

David began to pile up the drums. But there was a tramp asleep behind them. He was angry.

"I don't come in your place, moving all the things around, do I?" he shouted at them. They ran.

"We go ask Lesley," David said. "He did say he been up there."

Lesley's dad cleans windows when he is home. He keeps a long ladder in the back yard. He leaves it leaning against the viaduct.

And they all climbed up as easy as pie.

They walked high and happy among all the weeds flowering in the gravel, and even beginning trees growing there.

They could see down into all the yards.
They could see a man mending his shoe.

They could see a woman hanging out washing. They could look over the shiny slate roofs, and all the cracked black chimneys.

They walked and walked.

"Where we to?" said David in a while.

"Corner of Britannia Street," said Lesley. "You can see the Victoria Tavern. You see the green and brown tiles on that building? That's it."

"Not Britannia Street," said Dulcie. "We in a hanging garden. We in Babylon."

David began to sing, like they learned at the Sunday Mission. "*By the rivers of Babylon, where we sat down . . .*"

The others joined in. "*Where we sat down, there we wept, When we remembered Zion.*"

They all walked and sang

till the viaduct suddenly stopped. There is a broken arch there, hanging over the canal.

"What I tell you?" said Dulcie. "There the very waters, like it say in the song."

Then they three sat on the very edge, and looked right down over.

"Why they all weeping in that song?" said Lesley.

"I know that," said Dulcie. "Some bad old King took all the people out of their own place. He took them to Babylon, and he showed them the hanging gardens, and the lovely waters, but they were wanting to go home. They remembered Zion, where they from."

"If this is Babylon," said David, "where old Zion?"

"Zion is in Africa, my dad say, We all come from there," said Lesley.

"That all too long ago to weep for," said David. "Back home in Jamaica is where I think of. Man, do you remember salt fish on Sunday, and rice with peas?"

"It's nice here," said Dulcie. "I can see the gasholder all swaying upside down in the water."

"You remember the dark green glossy trees, and the old tree frog flopping on your feet when you walk out at night? Always the fool cicadas come bombing in through the open door," said Lesley.

"I bet there are frogs right down there in the canal," said Dulcie. "I bet they come out at night, and croak something frightful!"

"And the red'n'black bus with all the things from the market piled on top, going uphill home," said David.

"When I think of that, I surely could weep," said Lesley.

But he was smiling. It was Dulcie who felt sad.
"I always been here," she said. "I ain't got no Zion."

Back along the viaduct, she felt sad all the way.

On the way back from Lesley's house, they met David's mumma. She was shopping at the street market, buying sweet potatoes for David's supper.

"What you all been doing?" she asked.

"We been to Babylon," David told her. "Up along the viaduct. We walked and walked."

"Oh my!" said David's mumma. "Now you listen here.
You not to do anything foolish. If you go again, you do be
most careful not to fall off!"

"I'm not going again," Dulcie told her. "Babylon ain't no
fun without you got Zion to weep for. I always been here. I
ain't got no place else to weep for."

"Don't you worry about that, Dulcie lamb!" said David's mumma. "Don't matter where you been, or where you never been, you surely will have something to weep for, by and by."

"Will I?" said Dulcie.

"Oh my!" said David's mumma. "Yes you will!"

So Dulcie cheered up. She ran home happy.
She ran home all along below the viaduct, singing all the way.